This book belongs to

....

First published in 2025
Text copyright© Cheryl Austin
Illustrastion copyright © Samantha Sykes
All rights reserved

ISBN 978-1-0369-1627-5

A llama is strolling along in the beautiful sunshine when she notices a flamingo sitting in the reeds. She approaches her and says hello.

"Hello, I'm Lara the llama, what is your name?"

"Hello, I'm Tiny the flamingo."

Tiny and Lara become best friends and decide to go on a picnic together.

Tiny starts standing up to go on the picnic with her new friend.

Lara stares at Tiny for a long time with a confused expression on her face. She cannot believe her eyes! She asks...

"Tiny, why are you called Tiny when you are so big?"

Tiny expresses that she doesn't know why she is called Tiny and asks her new friend...

"Why are you called Lara?"

Lara explains that she is called Lara because she is a llama and that also begins with a 'L' and that Tiny needs to find out the reason for her name.

Tiny starts her new quest, searching for the reason for her name.

Tiny bumps into her Uncle Freddie.

"Hello, Uncle Freddie, do you know why
I am called Tiny when I am so big?"

Uncle Freddie replies
"I don't know why you are called Tiny."

Uncle Freddie suggests that she
should go and ask her cousin Florence.

Tiny continues her quest, searching for the reason for her name.

"Hello Tiny, do you want to play with me?" asks Florence.

Tiny tells her that she cannot play at the moment because she is on a quest to find out the reason for her name.

She asks Florence "Do you know why I am called Tiny when I am so big?"

Florence replies "I don't know why you are called Tiny when you are so big, maybe go and ask your brother."

Tiny continues her quest, searching for the reason for her name.

"Hi Finley, I am in such a hurry because I am on a very important quest."

Finley gets very excited and asks Tiny if he can help her on her quest.

Tiny asks her brother "Do you know why I am called Tiny when I am so big?"

Finley replies "Ahhhh sorry Tiny, I don't know why you are called Tiny when you are soooooooo big!"

Finley recommends Tiny to go and ask their mummy.

Tiny continues her quest, searching for the reason for her name.

Tiny finally finds her mummy and tells her all about her quest, trying to find out the reason for her name.

Tiny asks her mummy
"Why am I called Tiny when I am soooooooo big?"

Mummy giggles and explains to Tiny that she is called Tiny because she was the smallest egg out of all her brothers and sisters.

Her mummy also tells her that she thought that she would be a very, very, very tiny flamingo.

Tiny said "I am not very tiny though, I am the BIGGEST and BRIGHTEST flamingo ever!"

Mummy replies "I know, Tiny, that is what makes you and your name so special."

Mummy and Tiny hug and smile at each other, Tiny feels really happy because she has completed her quest and found out the reason for her name.

3 fun and fantastic facts about flamingos

Fun fact 1: Flamingos are social birds that live in colonies called Flamboyances.

Fun fact 2: Flamingos build nests from mud.

Fun fact 3: Baby flamingos are born grey or white.

3 Quick Quests for you and your family to complete

Quick quest 1: Can you find out the reason for your name?

Quick quest 2: Can you find the hidden pink flamingo feathers throughout the story?

Quick quest 3: Can you look for a flamingo in your own surroundings?
Maybe at home, at school or on a walk.

Lara the llama continues on her stroll ...